Teggs is no ordinary ~~~~
he's an astrosaur!

Captain of the amazing spaceship DSS *Sauropod*, he goes on dangerous missions, fighting evil with the help of his faithful crew, Gipsy, Arx, and Iggy!

Don't miss the Astrosaurs' other adventures!

Book Two: *The Hatching Horror*

Book Three: *The Seas of Doom*
Coming October 2006

ASTROSAURS
BOOK ONE

Riddle
of the
Raptors

BY STEVE COLE

ILLUSTRATED BY CHARLIE FOWKES

Aladdin Paperbacks
New York • London • Toronto • Sydney

This book is a work of fiction. Any references to historical events, real people, or real locales are used fictitiously. Other names, characters, places, and incidents are the product of the author's imagination, and any resemblance to actual events or locales or persons, living or dead, is entirely coincidental.

ALADDIN PAPERBACKS
An imprint of Simon & Schuster Children's Publishing Division
1230 Avenue of the Americas, New York, NY 10020
Text copyright © 2005 by Steve Cole
Illustrations copyright © 2005 by Charlie Fowkes
Originally published in Great Britain in 2005 by Red Fox, an imprint of Random House Children's Books
Published by arrangement with Rocket Editorial Ltd.
First U.S. edition 2006
All rights reserved, including the right of reproduction in whole or in part in any form.
ALADDIN PAPERBACKS and colophon are trademarks of Simon & Schuster, Inc.
Designed by Steve Kennedy
The text of this book was set in ITC Legacy Serif Book.
Manufactured in the United States of America
First Aladdin Paperbacks edition June 2006
10 9 8 7 6 5 4 3 2 1
Library of Congress Control Number 2005934207
ISBN-13: 978-0-689-87841-1
ISBN-10: 0-689-87841-9

For Tobey

WARNING!

THINK YOU KNOW ABOUT DINOSAURS?

THINK AGAIN!

The dinosaurs . . .

Big, stupid lumbering reptiles. Right?

All they did was eat, sleep, and roar a bit. Right?

Died out millions of years ago when a big meteor struck Earth. Right?

Wrong!

The dinosaurs weren't stupid. They may have had small brains, but they used them well. They had big thoughts and big dreams.

By the time the meteor hit, the last dinosaurs had already left Earth forever. Some species had discovered how to travel through space as early as the Triassic period, and were already enjoying a new life among the stars.

No one has found evidence of dinosaur technology yet. But the first fossil bones were found only in 1787, and new finds are being made all the time. The proof is out there, buried in the ground.

And the dinosaurs live on, way out in space, even now. They've settled down in a place they call the Jurassic Quadrant, and over the last sixty-five million years they've continued to evolve. . . .

The dinosaurs we'll be meeting are part of a special group called the Dinosaur Space

Service. Their job is to explore space, to go on exciting missions, and to fight evil and protect the innocent!

These heroic herbivores are not just dinosaurs.

They are *astrosaurs*!

NOTE: The following story has been translated from secret Dinosaur Space Service records. Earthling dinosaur names are used throughout, although some changes have been made for easy reading.

THE CREW OF THE DSS SAUROPOD

Teggs Stegosaur,
Captain

Arx Orano,
First Officer

Gipsy Saurine,
Communications
Officer

Iggy Tooth,
Chief Engineer

Jurassic Quadrant

Ankylos

Steggos

Diplox

INDEPENDENT
DINOSAUR
ALLIANCE

vegetarian
sector

Squawk
Major

DSS
UNION OF
PLANETS

PETROSAURIA

Corytho

Lambeos

Cry

Tri System

Iguanos

Aqua Minor

SEA R

OUTER SPACE

Geldos Cluster

Teerex Major

Olympus

TYRANNOSAUR TERRITORIES

carnivore sector

Raptos

Planet Sixty

THEROPOD EMPIRE

Megalos

vegmeat zone
(neutral space)

TILE SPACE

Pliosaur Nurseries

Not to scale

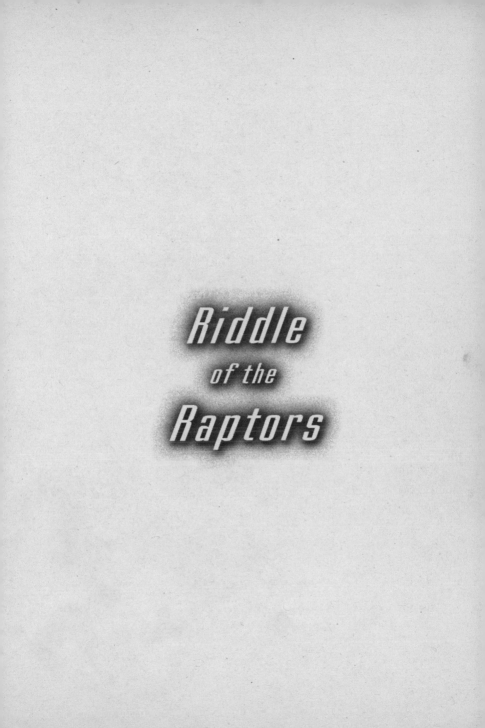

Riddle
of the
Raptors

Chapter One

THE ADVENTURE BEGINS

Space. It stretched on forever.

Distant stars twinkled. Comets showed off their sparkling tails. Strange planets hung like bright bulbs in the black sky.

Teggs Stegosaur stared out at it all in wonder. He was standing on the top deck of a massive space station—the headquarters of the Dinosaur Space Service.

At last, he thought. *After years of training, I've made it. I'm an* astrosaur! He frowned. *But why have I been asked to come to headquarters alone? I hope I haven't messed up already!*

Just then, a small pterosaur flapped noisily down the corridor toward him. "Admiral Rosso will see you now," he squawked. "Follow me! Follow me!"

Teggs gulped, and lumbered after the flying reptile on his four squat, scaly legs. He was a handsome orange-brown stegosaurus, eight meters long from the point of his beak to the tip of his spiny tail. A line of armored plates ran down his scaly back like a dozen small sails.

The pterosaur perched just outside the admiral's office. "In you go," he screeched. "In you go!"

Teggs pushed through the heavy jungle vines that hung down over the doorway. Like all dinosaur technology, the space station had been *grown*, not built. The floor was thick with juicy moss, and the walls were bright with flowers and fruits. Here and there tall, thick tree trunks stretched up to the high grassy ceiling. Astrosaurs always kept plenty of plants around the place, and not just because they were good to eat. Their space-ships ran on dung, so every meal meant a little more fuel for the engines.

"Ah! Young Teggs!" boomed Admiral Rosso from behind a vast wooden desk. He was the crusty old barosaurus in charge of the Dinosaur Space Service. "Thank you for coming."

Teggs carefully raised his front legs in a dinosaur salute. "You wanted to see me, sir?"

"I wanted to congratulate you," said the admiral, smiling. His scaly head bobbed about on a neck as long as a fireman's hose—and ten times thicker. "You have passed your final Space Service tests with a record-breaking score. You are without doubt the bravest, most daring—and *hungriest*—astrosaur ever to train here."

Teggs blushed and quickly swallowed the mouthful of ferns he'd pulled from the floor. "Thank you, sir. Er, sorry for eating your office, sir."

"Nothing wrong with a hearty appetite," the admiral said, and chuckled. "But I think it's *adventure* you're truly hungry for."

Teggs grinned. "My stomach's rumbling at the thought of it!"

"That's why I'm putting you in charge of your very own spaceship," said the admiral. "I'm making you a captain!"

"Captain? And my very own spaceship?" Teggs's beak dropped open in amazement. This was a dream come true.

The admiral pulled aside a curtain of jungle creepers to reveal a window. Through it Teggs saw an amazing spaceship. It was shaped like an enormous egg, with six thick prongs sticking out. At the end of every prong sat a slightly smaller egg. These were the shuttles.

Teggs whistled in wonder. "That's *my* ship?"

"That's her." The admiral beamed. "The DSS *Sauropod*, finest in the entire Dinosaur Space Service. That ship—and you, Captain Teggs—

have been chosen for a very important mission." He unrolled some star charts with his long tail. "Recognize this?"

"That's the Jurassic Quadrant," said Teggs. "The part of space we call home." He pointed to one half of it with a tail spike. "Those green planets are in the Vegetarian Sector. The red ones are where the carnivores live."

"Yes, those mean old meat-eaters," said the admiral. "We've all come a long way from dear old Earth. Such a shame that beastly space rock walloped into it."

"Yes, sir." Teggs shuddered. If the dinosaurs hadn't discovered space travel before the meteor hit, they'd all have been wiped out! "Do you think anyone will ever live on Earth again, sir?"

"Who knows," sighed the admiral. "But we dinosaurs have thrived in outer space. Earth is just a tiny speck compared to the vastness of the Jurassic Quadrant!"

Teggs nodded keenly. "And there's still so much of it to explore!"

"That's where you come in," said the admiral. "You're now a fully trained astrosaur captain. Your mission is to explore space in the DSS *Sauropod*. To go in peace . . . to spread the way of the plant-eater . . . to keep an eye on those greedy meat-eaters . . . and to protect our people, wherever they may be."

Teggs nodded even *more* keenly. "I'll need a crew," he said.

"I've already got you one." The admiral swatted a button on the wall with his tail, and the window turned into a scanner screen.

It showed a picture of a gray triceratops with three proud horns and a parrotlike beak.

"This is Arx Orano," said the admiral. "He's a very well-respected astrosaur. He'll be your first officer."

Teggs smiled. Then the image changed to show a pretty duck-billed dinosaur, striped black and white all over.

"This is your com-
munications officer,
Gipsy Saurine," said
the admiral. "You can
see from her snout
that she's a hadrosaur.
Her mind's as sharp as
a raptor's claw, and she
loves a challenge." He smiled. "That's why I've put her on *your* ship!"

"I'm glad to have her on board," said Teggs.

The picture changed again. Now it showed a tough-looking iguanodon on his hind legs. His arms were thick and strong. Instead of thumbs he had wicked bony spikes.

"And this is Iggy Tooth," said the admiral, "a top engineer. He can turn a clawful of scrap into a space motor before you can say 'ornithomimosaur.'"

Teggs gulped. He wasn't sure he could say that at all.

"He's also very good in battle," the admiral said. "So if you ever find trouble—find Iggy fast!"

"I will," said Teggs grimly. "So, when am I off on these exciting missions?"

"Oh, soon. Very soon." The admiral cleared his throat. "But there's a little something I need you to do first. . . ."

Chapter Two

BATTLE STATIONS!

"A taxi service!" huffed Captain Teggs for the hundredth time. "The finest ship in the fleet, the best crew . . . and the admiral turns us into a taxi service!"

Gipsy turned her long, flat snout toward him. "Not just *any* taxi service, Captain," she reminded him. "We're in charge of the Vegetarian

Sector's top athletes. We'll get them to the Great Dinosaur Games in style!"

Arx nodded his frilly head. "It's the biggest space sports contest *ever*. Every species in the quadrant is coming to Olympus for the games. And when those miserable meat-eaters see the DSS *Sauropod* arrive, think how impressed they'll be!"

"I suppose so." Teggs chewed grumpily on some ferns from the wall of his control pit. "How long before we arrive?"

"Right now we're just passing the moons of Minnos," said Gipsy. "That's the halfway point. Then, once we've swung round Planet Sixty, it's straight on to Olympus. We should arrive tomorrow night."

"And the games start the day after!" Arx added.

"And nothing to do until then," sighed Teggs. "I was hoping for a little more action—"

Ka-Boom! The whole ship shook with an enormous explosion.

Teggs spat out his beakful of plants and jumped up from the control pit. "What was *that*?" he bellowed.

"Warning! Warning!" The shriek of the alarm pterosaur echoed out from every speaker on the ship.

"Unknown invaders coming aboard!"

Arx swung his great head round to his instruments. "Someone's blown a hole in our ship!"

"On our first-ever flight?" cried Gipsy. "That's not fair!"

"I wanted action," Teggs muttered. "And I guess I've got it!"

"Red alert!" The alarm pterosaur squawked even louder. "Raptors on board! Repeat—*raptors on board*!"

"Battle stations!" Teggs roared. "Gipsy, where *are* these raptors?"

"The hole's on level seven, Captain," Gipsy reported. "It's close to the relaxation room." Then the crest of her scaly face flushed bright blue with worry. "Uh-oh. That's where the athletes are!"

"We have to drive these raptors off the ship—*fast*," said Teggs. "Arx, get Iggy on it!"

Arx jabbed the communicator with his nose

horn. "Iggy!" he snapped. "Raptor invaders on level seven. Our athletes are in danger. Prepare for battle!"

"Switch on the scanners, Gipsy," Teggs ordered.

At first they could only see the rocky moons of Minnos. Then a sinister craft came into view, hanging in space like a giant ivory tooth.

"A raptor death-ship!" cried Gipsy. "We've flown into an ambush!"

Suddenly another big explosion sent the *Sauropod* spinning. Teggs's seven-ton body was rolled over and over until he smashed into the thick plant-life that covered the nearest wall.

His team of tiny flying reptiles—fifty daring dimorphodon—flapped wildly around the flight deck, trying to sort out the damage. They bashed the controls with their beaks and yanked on levers with tough bony claws.

Arx rose from the grassy floor and checked his instruments. "There are *five* death-ships out there! They were hiding behind the moons. Now we're surrounded!"

"Put up the shields!" Teggs yelled. "And fetch me my armor!"

The dimorphodon crew rushed to obey. In moments four of the flapping reptiles were fitting Teggs into his head and tail armor. "I'll join the fight with Iggy down below," he said. "Arx, Gipsy, try to get us out of here."

"Understood, Captain," barked Arx. The dimorphodon team leaders flapped down to perch on Arx's head, ready to take his commands.

Gipsy looked at Teggs. "Be careful, sir," she said.

As the moss-lined elevator heaved down to the crew decks, Teggs heard the sound of fighting growing louder. He gritted his teeth. The spines that ran along his arched back turned a deep, warning red.

"I'll get those raptors," he muttered fiercely. "They'll be sorry they stepped onto *my* ship!"

As the doors opened, Teggs sprang out, flexed the great spiked club of his armored tail, then charged along the corridor.

He found the battle raging ahead of him. The air was thick with shrieks and roars. Nimble velociraptors in full battle armor skipped around the heavier ankylosaurs blocking their way. A dozen iguanodon reared up on their hind legs, roaring. Their claws ended in metal tips that fired stun rays into the raptor ranks. But the beams of light bounced off the raptors' chest plates and helmets. Teggs's ears rang with *thwacks* and *thuds* as his crew's heavy tails swiped through the air at their attackers.

Iggy Tooth was in the thick of the fighting. He caught sight of Teggs and swiftly saluted. "Set your stun claws to maximum, boys!" Iggy cried, a blur of green scales as he dodged his way through the fighting, keeping perfect balance with his short, stiff tail. "The captain's come to join us! We can't lose now!"

But even as he spoke, two raptors finally managed to tear straight past the massive ankylosaur that barred their way. They bared their bloodred teeth at Teggs.

"Sssurrender your ship, Captain," hissed the largest of the two raptors as they advanced with razor-sharp claws. "Or you shall die!"

Chapter Three

KIDNAPPED!

Teggs shook his head and sneered at the approaching raptors. "I'm not ready to become a stego-burger just yet," he growled. "And it'll take more than a couple of corny carnivores like you to take my ship!"

Teggs lashed out with his armored tail and sent the first raptor flying. The second brought his jaws down hard on the spiky, bonelike club at the tail's end. It was a bad move. A second later every tooth in his ugly head was broken and raining down to the mossy floor.

The
furious
carnivore
gnashed his
gums and turned
to his fallen mate.
"Ssstop him!"

The first raptor leaped
forward once more to
bite Teggs on the neck. Teggs quickly ducked
down and turned with surprising speed, so
that his attacker smacked into his back. The
raptor toppled backward and landed on top
of his friend.

Teggs prepared to fight his way through to
Iggy. But then a strange wailing noise started
up. At once the raptors broke off from the
battle and backed off.

"You hear that, boys?" cried Iggy triumphantly. "That's the raptor retreat signal! They're giving up! Come on, let's see them off the ship!"

As Iggy's battle squad charged off after the retreating raptors, Teggs pressed his head up against the communicator. "Captain to flight deck. Well done, crew. We've scared them off! The raptors are running away!"

But Arx sounded worried. "I don't think we *did* scare them off, Captain," he said. "We only fired off two laser bolts, and the raptor ships didn't even fire back."

Teggs thought hard. "You know, you might be right," he said slowly. "Those soldiers gave up pretty easily too. One minute they wanted me to surrender the *Sauropod*—the next they were retreating back to their ships as fast as their claws would carry them."

Gipsy's voice sounded over the speaker. "Perhaps they only retreated because they'd got what they came for. . . ."

"Of course!" Teggs grunted and charged off down the corridor after Iggy. The raptors didn't really want to take the ship at all. They'd started the fight just to keep Teggs and his crew busy—while they went after the athletes.

"They must be planning to ruin the Great Dinosaur Games!" he cried. "But surely they wouldn't *dare* eat our greatest athletes!"

Teggs charged into the *Sauropod*'s enormous

relaxation room. It was like a miniature forest, with an enormous crystal clear bathing pool in its center. Ordinarily the dinosaur athletes would've been chewing and resting or splashing about. But right now they were all cowering behind a large saltasaurus wrestler in the corner.

"Are they gone?" whimpered a maiasaura

shot-putter, his belly pressed low against the grass so that he could barely be seen.

"Yes, they've gone back to their ships," said Teggs. "I was worried they'd taken all of you with them!"

"No way," said the saltasaurus, the bumps on her hide bristling. "Two raptors looked in here, but I scared them off."

"I see," said Teggs doubtfully. He knew that raptors didn't scare easily. "Is anyone missing?"

"Wait! The stegoceras aren't here," cried the shot-putter. "They were in the showers when the alarms sounded."

"Oh, no!" Teggs groaned. He charged back down the corridor and through the doors to the showers. Then he stuck his head inside. "Anyone there?" he asked as he peered through the steam.

But his only answer was the mournful drip of water onto the floor. There was no sign of the stegoceras athletes. The showers were empty.

Teggs stomped back to the communicator in the wall. "Captain to flight deck," he growled. "You were right, Arx. This wasn't just a raid. It was a *kidnapping*!"

Chapter Four

A DEADLY MESSAGE

Captain Teggs sat tensely in his control pit, chewing on twigs.

Arx had found images of the two stegoceras, and Gipsy had put them on the scanner. The athletes were perky orange creatures, each about the size of a goat. One was named Hank, the other Crank. They had feeble forearms and long straight tails, and ran about on two legs. But their heads were truly eye-catching: a solid lump of bone the size of a football bulged above their snouts.

"What sport do they play?" wondered Gipsy.

"They were hot tips to win the head-butting contest," Arx said.

"I'm an idiot!" sighed Teggs. "Two days until the Great Dinosaur Games, and I let a bunch of raptors sneak on board and take our best butters. I must have a brain the size of a Ping-Pong ball!"

Arx cleared his throat. "Er, you *do* have a brain the size of a Ping-Pong ball, Captain," he said delicately. "You know, being a stegosaurus and all."

"So I do!" said Teggs, cheering up a bit. "I shouldn't be so hard on myself."

Just then, Teggs's personal communicator beeped.

"Uh-oh," he said. "Here's someone who *will* be hard on me. It's Admiral Rosso!"

"Captain Teggs!" boomed Admiral Rosso. "I've read your report. I can hardly believe what has happened. It's a disaster! A mess! A total foul-up!"

"I'm sorry, sir," said Teggs. "Perhaps . . . perhaps I'm just not good enough to be captain of the *Sauropod*."

"Piffle," said the admiral sternly. "Everyone makes mistakes, Captain. It's how you make up for them that counts." He paused. "Just make sure you sort out *this* mistake fast—before the Great Dinosaur Games begin!"

The communicator switched off.

"Are you all right, Captain?" asked Arx gently.

"Never mind me," said Teggs. "It's those poor stegoceras athletes I'm worried about!"

Gipsy raised her snout in the air and whistled and hooted at the dimorphodon flight crew. A few of them flapped down at once and massaged their captain's spiky back with their claws. "So, what do we do now?" she asked.

Iggy was pacing up and down the flight deck in a foul temper, clicking his thumb spikes. "I say we hunt down these velociraptor vermin and *make* them give us back our athletes!"

"The Jurassic Quadrant is a big area to search," Arx reminded him.

"Why did they take only the head-butters, out of everyone on board?" wondered Gipsy.

"You've got something there!" Teggs rose up suddenly, and the dimorphodon flapped off in fright. "The raptors looked in the athletes' room, but kept searching till they found the stegoceras in the showers. Why?"

"Well, if the raptors *have* taken the stegoceras for a reason," Arx said, "we can only wait and see if they tell us what it is."

There was a sudden creaking and squeaking noise from Gipsy's communications console. "I'm getting a message, Captain. Picture and sound," she reported briskly, checking the readout. "It's from a raptor!"

"Put it on the scanner," Teggs ordered.

The screen showed the hateful features of a big scaly raptor. Clearly he had been in many battles over the years. His pointed jaw was scuffed and scraped, and he wore a black eye patch over one eye.

"I am General Loki," said the raptor in a silky smooth whisper. "Commander of the Seven Fleets of Death! Ruler of the meat mines of Raptos! Eater of edmontosaurus, devourer of diplodocus—"

"And all-round pain in the tail," Teggs cut in before the raptor got really carried away. He had heard of General Loki—the nastiest, meanest velociraptor in the Jurassic Quadrant. "At least you've got less of a lisp than your raptor crew. What do you want?"

Loki narrowed his one remaining eye. "It's

what *you* want that we should be discussing, Captain Teggs. . . ." Loki moved aside from the scanner cameras to reveal the two stegoceras athletes hunched up behind him. Both of them had grubby bandages wrapped round their heads.

"Hank! Crank!" Teggs reared up out of his control pit. "Are you okay?"

"We're cool!" Hank and Crank chorused, and lightly tapped their heads together as if to prove it. "Ouch!" they both yelled.

Gipsy frowned. "Have the raptors hurt you?"

"Nah," said Hank. "We just woke up with a headache." He waved his feeble forearm at his bandage. "Look! Some raptor doctors checked us out, then gave us these headbands!"

Crank nodded enthusiastically. "Cool or what!"

The stegoceras were about to bash heads again when two raptor guards restrained them.

Loki came back into view. "So you see, Captain," he said, "your athletes are fit and well. And they'll stay that way if you agree to our terms."

Teggs glared at him. "And just what exactly *are* your terms?"

"You must pay us a billion pieces of purest gold!" Loki laughed nastily. "And if you refuse, *your* athletes become *my* supper!"

Chapter Five

SHOWDOWN ON PLANET SIXTY

Iggy, Arx, Teggs, and Gipsy stared at one another in disbelief.

"A billion pieces?" Teggs spluttered. "You're crazy! It would take *years* to gather all that gold!"

"Oh. Really?" Loki looked a little downcast, and clicked his claws. "All right then . . . call it twenty."

"Twenty?" echoed Teggs.

Loki nodded. "But throw in a nice flat-screen satellite monitor, too. Mine has just broken."

Iggy, Arx, Teggs, and Gipsy stared at one another once again, in still deeper disbelief.

"From a billion pieces . . . to twenty?" Teggs started counting on his toes, then frowned. "That *is* quite a drop, isn't it?"

"Raptors are awful at doing deals, Captain," Arx said in a low voice. "They normally sort out any squabbles by biting each other."

"Mind you," said Iggy grudgingly, "that Loki's smarter than he looks. Those flat-screen satellite monitors are brilliant!"

"Oh, and we want some moss, too," Loki added as if the thought had just occurred to him. "It goes so well with raw apatosaurus."

He licked his leathery lips with a forked tongue. "The exchange will be made at noon tomorrow on Planet Sixty."

Teggs frowned. "Planet Sixty? Isn't that on the way to Olympus?"

"Yes, Captain," said Arx. "It's a small swampy planet just outside the Vegetarian Sector. It's so dull, no one could be bothered to name it!"

Loki smiled. "I trust your . . . *flimsy* new ship can reach Planet Sixty in time."

Teggs narrowed his eyes. "We'll be there."

"Splendid. But no tricks," said the grizzled general. "You're to come unarmed, Captain, with just one member of your crew. Until tomorrow . . ." He nodded his head in farewell, and the screen went blank.

"What do we do, Captain?" asked Gipsy.

"What *can* we do?" Teggs uprooted a fern from the floor and chewed it grumpily. "You heard the admiral. We need to sort this out fast. Next stop, Planet Sixty—full speed ahead!"

And so the *Sauropod* sailed through space toward the pickup point.

"Planet Sixty is coming into range, Captain,"

announced Gipsy at last. She blinked her wide eyes at him. "Iggy says the shuttle is ready to depart."

Teggs came out of the control pit. "Those raptors are up to something," he said. "I feel it in my tail spikes."

As he stomped off toward the shuttle, Teggs had an uneasy feeling that something was badly wrong. He felt naked without his electro-tail armor. He bet Iggy felt the same without his stun claws. But Loki had insisted they come unarmed. Teggs couldn't risk crossing him while he held the two athletes.

Even so—would the raptors keep their side of the bargain?

Iggy saluted Teggs as he came aboard the shuttle. "Dung burners set to maximum, Captain!"

"Okay." Teggs nodded. "Blast off!"

The shuttle—shaped like a giant egg with two noisy motors on the fat end—shuddered and

shook as the
power began to
build. The engines
ignited, and the sweet
smell of dinosaur manure
filled the air as the shuttle thundered away into
space.

Within minutes they
were flying through the
grotty green skies of
Planet Sixty. Soon, with
a slithering bump and a rattling roar, the shuttle skidded to a stop on the swampy surface.

Teggs opened the doors and led the way outside. Iggy waddled close behind him, carrying
the ransom on his back.

They hadn't walked far before they saw the
raptor death-shuttle—an enormous pointed
spike with a bloodred tip. Next to it stood
General Loki and three of his raptor guards,

who were watching over the athletes with hungry eyes.

"Welcome, Captain," sneered Loki. He eyed the bundle on Iggy's back. "You have met my demands, I see."

"Let's just get this over with," said Teggs. He swished his enormous tail from side to side menacingly. "Give us back our athletes!"

With a hiss the raptor guards herded the stegoceras over to Teggs. One of the guards came toward Iggy, her claws raised and ready to slash. She cut clean through the thick twine that bound the ransom bundle to the iguanodon's back, and paraded the package back to her ship triumphantly.

Teggs peered at the athletes with their band-aged heads. "You two okay?"

"We're cool," said Hank.

"Just glad to be out of that flea pit," added Crank, nodding at the raptor shuttle.

"Farewell, Captain!" called Loki. "Enjoy the Great Dinosaur Games! I'm sure they'll go off with a bang!" With a nasty chuckle he scuttled into his ship, which took off at once.

"Good riddance!" yelled Crank.

"Totally," Hank said, and nodded. "That ship stank of meat, man!" He tried to mime being suffocated, but his little forearms couldn't reach his neck.

"Wait a second," Iggy said gruffly. His nostrils were twitching. "Did either of you *sit* in any of that meat?"

Hank and Crank shook their bandaged heads.

Teggs sniffed the air, and wrinkled his snout. "I can smell it too. . . ."

Suddenly the swampy ground began to shake. "What's that?" Hank squeaked.

"Something big," shouted Iggy, looking around as the pounding on the ground got louder. "Coming this way!"

Teggs lumbered up a small hill to see what it was—and froze in his tracks.

A terrifying creature was bounding up toward him—a real giant, at least three times the size of Teggs. He stood upright on powerful legs as big as tree trunks. His massive mouth brimmed with daggerlike teeth. Hot on his scaly heels, another ten of the monsters were approaching fast.

"Back to the ship, quick!" called Teggs as he thundered back down the hill. *"There are* T. rexes *on this planet!"*

Chapter Six

DANGEROUS FLIGHT

Teggs led the charge back to the shuttle. The ground shook as if it were going to open up beneath their feet. *T. rex*es didn't normally hunt in packs—unless they were scouting out new planets to take over.

"You're welcome to this dump," muttered Teggs. Then he skidded to a halt. Iggy and the others almost crashed into him.

Another *T. rex*, the biggest yet, was looming over their shuttle.

Teggs squared up to the ferocious carnivore. "Iggy, I'll lead her away. Get those athletes inside the ship!"

Iggy hesitated. "But, Captain—"

"Do it!" growled Teggs.

He ran to the edge of a cliff, and the *T. rex* chased after him. Then Teggs faced up to the monster. He swung his tail around so fast that the spikes on the end of it became an ivory blur.

The terrifying tyrannosaur roared and lunged forward, but Teggs's tail whacked her on the side of her head. Staggering sideways in surprise, the *T. rex* fell over the edge of the cliff and into the swamp below.

But there was no time to celebrate. Teggs rushed back to the shuttle—and the whole snarling gang of *T. rex*es was now blocking his way.

"This *our* planet," growled their leader. "You in big trouble, Plant-boy."

"We were just visiting," Teggs told her. "We'll be off now. Leave you to it."

The *T. rex* shook her head. "No."

"Er, can't we talk about this?" asked Teggs hopefully, edging toward the shuttle.

"No," she said.

Teggs suddenly remembered what his astrosaur trainer had taught him: *T. rex*es hate talking. They've never learned how to do it properly. Ten seconds into a conversation, and they usually eat the dinosaur they're speaking to.

"We HUNGRY!" roared the *T. rex* leader. She opened her jaws and lunged at Teggs. He rolled clear just in time—and the creature crunched down on one of the shuttle's motors. Her teeth tore the engine clear off.

"Take off, Iggy!" yelled Teggs. "Never mind

me! With only one engine you'll have a bumpy ride, but you might just make it!"

The *T. rex* leader roared in anger. The engine was jammed in her mouth. She lumbered toward Teggs and tried to stamp on his tail.

Teggs backed away. "Missed me, loser!" he called bravely. But deep down he knew there was no hope of escape. Already the other tyrannosaurs were drawing closer, roaring and snapping their gruesome jaws. . . .

The shuttle still hadn't taken off. Teggs guessed Iggy couldn't bring himself to leave his captain behind.

"Go *now*, Iggy!" he yelled. "That's an order!"

"Aye, aye, Captain," said Iggy sadly.

The shuttle's remaining engine burst into life— and made a *very* rude noise. The *T. rexes* all turned round in shock.

While they were distracted, Teggs pushed past them. The shuttle doors heaved open and he leaped inside, scattering the stegoceras like scaly bowling pins.

"Welcome back, Captain!" Iggy yelled, beaming.

"You didn't make that dreadful noise, did you?" gasped Teggs, warily sniffing the air.

"Not me!" said Iggy, revving the engine. "There must have been a buildup of dung gas trapped in the exhaust pipe. It's clear now."

Teggs sighed. "If only *we* were clear of these *T. rex*es."

The shuttle took off wonkily. It was meant to fly with two engines, not one. Unbalanced, it started to spin.

"Cool!" yelled Hank and Crank happily, as if it were a fairground ride. The shuttle bumped and bounced against the ground, and soon the ship's floor was flooded with swamp muck.

"I can't control it!" Iggy shouted.

To Teggs's dismay the *T. rex*es were running after the spinning shuttle.

"They're catching up!" yelled Crank.

The *T. rex*es loomed up, gnashing their jaws in triumph—all except their leader, who still had a mouthful of engine. The shuttle made another rude noise as it dipped down again.

"I know how you feel," muttered Teggs.

Then, suddenly, his little brain was filled with a big idea.

"There's just one chance," Teggs cried. He scavenged through the swamp muck until he found a big sharp stone. "Try to hold her steady, Iggy!" he yelled. Then he picked up the stone with his beak and tossed it in the air.

With a noise like a whip crack his tail lashed out and struck the stone, sending it flying out through the shuttle's doors.

The stone smacked against the engine caught in the *T. rex* leader's teeth. With a fiery bang the engine exploded!

The *T. rex* fell backward with an angry roar

of pain. And to everyone's amazement the other *T. rex*es toppled over too!

Iggy hooted for joy. "What happened, Captain? What did you do?"

"The rude noise reminded me—our engines run on gas made by burning dung," said Teggs. "The engines are full to bursting with gas! And that gas is explosive stuff."

"It sure is!" Iggy grinned. "There's a lot to be said for a good, healthy vegetarian diet!"

Hank and Crank clapped their tiny hands together with glee.

"Awesome!" Hank laughed.

"The fumes alone were enough to knock those uglies out cold!" Crank added.

Just then, the shuttle's crazy course smoothed out. Iggy beamed at the others. "You know what? I think I'm learning to fly this thing with one engine!"

"Oh!" Hank looked crestfallen. "Can't you go back to shaking us round and nearly crashing, like before? That was the *best*!"

Teggs frowned. "You've had one knock on the head too many, Hank!"

The others all laughed, but Teggs had to force a smile. He felt strangely tense from tail

to toes. Why? The danger was all over now.
Wasn't it?

On board the raptor shuttle,
General Loki was rubbing
his hands with glee. "Every-
thing went exactly as
planned!" He chuckled.
"That idiot Teggs has
no idea what we're
really up to. . . ."

"Excuse me, your horrible-
nessss," rasped one raptor
warrior. "We have just de-
tected *T. rexes* on Planet
Sssixty."

"*T. rexes*?" Loki's single eye narrowed. "Why
didn't you check before? Those brutes could
have eaten the lot of us!" He swiped at the
warrior, who yelped and fell to the floor. "Did
that stupid stegosaurus get away safely?"

The raptor nodded quickly. "By the ssskin of his teeth."

"Good," said Loki. "I should hate for anything to happen to Captain Teggs." He chuckled nastily. "At least, not until he's done what we need him to do!"

Chapter Seven

MYSTERY

When it was learned that Captain Teggs had rescued the stegoceras athletes, there were celebrations all over the *Sauropod*.

The other athletes staged a big welcome-back party for Hank and Crank.

Admiral Rosso sent special congratulations—"I knew you could do it!"

The grateful organizers of the Great Dinosaur Games even offered Teggs and a guest two special seats in the royal paddock.

On the flight deck Teggs was still glowing with pride. Soon he would be mingling with royalty! The kings and queens of every dinosaur species would be watching the games. This was the first time they had all gathered together in one place. It was truly a special occasion.

Teggs was jolted from his thoughts by a sudden clattering and whistling from the flock of flying reptiles around him.

"We're now in orbit around Olympus, Captain," Gipsy translated. "I think the dimorphodon are as excited as we are!" She cleared her throat. "Er . . . have you decided who you're taking to the games?"

"Yes." Teggs beamed at the stripy hadrosaur. "You! We'll take a shuttle down to the stadium with the other athletes in about one hour's time."

Gipsy grinned. "Yes, sir."

But Teggs's good mood vanished when he saw Arx plodding over, shaking his horned head with worry.

"I've been studying all the data on our recent raptor adventures," said the triceratops. "And something's worrying me."

But before he could go on, the flight deck doors swept open to reveal Hank and Crank. Iggy stood proudly behind them.

"Welcome to the flight deck," said Teggs politely.

"We just realized that we never thanked you properly for paying the ransom to get us back," said Crank. "I bet it was a total fortune, right?"

Teggs and Arx swapped awkward looks.

"Er . . . ," Teggs began, "*kind of—*"

"That's weird," said Gipsy suddenly. "I'm picking up a strange signal. It's interfering with our communicators."

"Find out where the signal's coming from," Teggs ordered, instantly alert.

"Wow, a captain's work is never done, huh?" Hank grinned. "Sorry to bug you when you're busy. We'll catch you later at the games."

"Yeah!" said Crank. "We're going to crack some serious skull down there, Captain—just for you!"

With that the stegoceras athletes left the flight deck.

"Good lads," said Iggy quietly. "They'll do us herbivores proud!"

"That's funny, Captain," Gipsy reported. "The interference is clearing now. Just sort of fading away."

"Don't worry, Gipsy," said Teggs. "I'm sure it's nothing." He turned back to his first officer. "Now, what were you saying?"

"Listen, Captain," Arx said gravely, "I checked the records for all recent raptor ransom demands. General Loki's demand for twenty gold pieces, a satellite monitor, and some moss is actually the *lowest* ransom ever recorded."

"That monitor *was* a beauty, though," Iggy reminded them glumly.

Arx ignored him. "And remember when they got on board? They could've taken *all* the athletes. Why just take Hank and Crank?"

Teggs nodded slowly. "And if it was really money they were after, why not just steal it from the ship?"

"Why not, indeed," said Arx. "Those raptors had us at their mercy—but they just gave up and flew away."

"What about those *T. rex*es on Planet Sixty?" Iggy argued. "I bet Loki knew they were down there. He was leading us into a trap."

"I don't think so," said Arx. "The raptors and *T. rex*es are fierce enemies."

Gipsy frowned. "Hang on, why did he pick Planet Sixty at all? It's light-years away from the raptors' world."

"But very handy for us," said Arx, his horns

glinting in the light. "It's on our way to the Dinosaur Games."

"That's crazy!" cried Iggy. "Why would the raptors want to make things easy for us?"

"There can only be one answer," said Teggs impressively.

Everyone looked at him.

Teggs swallowed nervously in the sudden spotlight. "Er . . . because they *wanted* us to pick up the stegoceras athletes with no delays. They wanted us to get them to the games on time—whatever it took!"

Arx nodded. "I think you're right."

The dimorphodon flight crew clapped their leathery wings politely.

Iggy raised his voice over the applause.

"Well, I don't know what they were planning, but security at the games is too tight for any funny business. You can't sneak a single salted snail in there without the security guards knowing about it." He sighed. "I should know, I've tried it!"

"Maybe so," said Teggs, turning to Gipsy. "But I think it's time we checked out the raptors' enclosure on Olympus. We've got plenty of questions. Now it's time to get the answers!"

Chapter Eight

RUMBLING THE RAPTORS

Teggs and Gipsy took a shuttle down to the planet's surface at top speed, while Arx and Iggy stayed on board the *Sauropod*.

"No sign of any raptor death-ships in orbit," Arx's voice crackled from the communicator. "But the *Sauropod* is getting plenty of admiring looks from the other ships parked here!"

"So she should," said Teggs, grinning. "Keep an eye on things. Gipsy and I are going to head straight for the raptor enclosure."

"Good luck, sir," said Arx.

. . .

Teggs and Gipsy's royal passes got them swiftly through the crowds. No one dared to question where the two dinosaurs were going, and they soon reached the raptor enclosure.

This was where the raptors trained for the games. The rough floor was covered with bones and dark scraps. Teggs didn't want to examine them too closely. The whole place was sticky and shadowy, and it stank of raw meat.

"Quiet, isn't it?" Gipsy hissed.

"Too quiet," Teggs murmured uneasily. He hadn't expected to breeze straight to the heart of the raptors' den. They should have met *some* kind of resistance by now!

Teggs crept on down the corridors as quietly as a seven-ton animal *can* creep. He thought longingly of the golden seats waiting for them in the royal paddock, glinting in the warm light from the planet's six suns. But a niggling feeling in his heavy bones told him that something bad was going to happen very soon—and that they didn't have long to stop it.

Teggs came to a sudden halt. He'd heard something up ahead—a distant buzzing sound. At first it sounded like a swarm of bees, but then he realized it was the sound of a mighty audience clapping and cheering over TV speakers.

Shuffling forward, Teggs poked his head round the nearest open door, marked CENTRAL CONTROL. It was a large room with dark TV screens piled up along one wall. A raptor, wearing the peaked cap of a security guard, sat alone in a chair with his back to the screens. His eyes were glued to a broadcast of the games' opening ceremony on a large monitor.

Teggs cleared his throat. "What do you think you're doing, you sniveling security guard?" he yelled.

The raptor leaped in the air as though he had sat on a spike. "Just checking the ssstegocerasss were in position, sssir!" he hissed hurriedly.

"Oh, yes?" Teggs frowned at the raptor. "In position for what?"

But the raptor had realized he was not explaining himself to his boss, but to some stupid herbivore! "You'll never know," he rasped. Eyes narrowed, he scuttled forward and threw himself at Teggs's neck.

Luckily, Teggs ducked out of reach just in time. The raptor sailed out through the doorway and into the wall opposite. Gipsy jabbed the back of his neck with her big bill. The raptor collapsed, and she sat on him.

"Help!" he shrieked. "I can't move!"

"Answer the captain's questions and I'll sit somewhere else," said Gipsy sweetly.

"First question," said Teggs. "Where are all your raptor buddies?"

"Where it is sssafe," said the raptor smugly. Then he seemed to think he had said too much. "I mean—they are all out training, of courssse."

"Leaving only someone as dumb as you behind?" Teggs shook his head. "I don't think so. You raptors are up to something. You're working for General Loki, aren't you?"

"No way!" squealed the raptor. "I have never heard the name of our glorioussssly evil Commander of the Ssseven Fleetsss of Death, ruler of the meat mines of Raptosss, eater of edmontosssaurusss and devourer of . . . er . . . ever before in my life. Ever."

Teggs and Gipsy looked doubtfully at each other.

"Fibber," said Teggs.

The raptor gasped. "How did you know?"

Teggs smiled. "That satellite monitor you were watching. It's the one we gave you in return for Hank and Crank!"

"So, what have you done to them?" said Gipsy. "Come on, talk—or I'll jab you where it *really* hurts!"

"Don't, please!" yelped the guard. "I'm the only raptor left on the whole planet. Olympusss is doomed—thanks to your knuckleheaded friends!"

Teggs felt a shiver down his backbone. "What do you mean?"

"I mean," hissed the raptor nastily, "that when we kidnapped your athletesss, our doctors sssecretly placed a big bomb in their ssstupid skulls!"

"What?" gasped Gipsy.

The raptor nodded proudly. "When they bang their heads together hard enough, the bombs will go off—and the royal families of every dinosssaur species will be destroyed in a huge explosion!"

Teggs glared down at their prisoner. "You wouldn't dare! The whole quadrant would come after you for revenge!"

"But firssst there will be chaos," the raptor hissed. "While every dinosssaur weeps in shock, our battle fleet shall attack their worlds."

Gipsy swallowed hard. "Taken by surprise, they won't stand a chance!"

The raptor laughed. "General Loki shall rule over half the galaxy!" He stared up at Teggs, eyes gleaming under the peak of his cap. "And it's all down to *you*, Captain! By bringing those head-butters here, *you've* helped it happen!"

Chapter Nine

COUNTDOWN TO CARNAGE

"You're bluffing," Teggs decided. "Why should we believe you?"

"Captain," gasped Gipsy, her crest turning bright blue in alarm. "Remember that strange sig- nal I picked up on the flight deck?"

Teggs nodded. "Sure."

"The signal started when Hank and Crank entered the flight deck, and stopped again when they left!" she said. "Don't you see? Those head bombs must've caused it!"

"We're in trouble," Teggs groaned.

The raptor chuckled. Gipsy jabbed her bill against the back of his head again, and he fell silent.

Teggs turned up the volume on the satellite monitor. The commentator speaking was a brachiosaurus with a neck so long he could oversee the entire sprawling stadium.

"For the first time in fifty years the royal families of every dinosaur species have been brought together," he said seriously. *"A spirit of friendly competition fills the air. Plant-eaters and carnivores stand side by*

side in perfect peace. Of course, that big wire fence between them helps. . . ."

"How long before the games begin?" asked Gipsy.

"It's almost three o'clock—almost time for the first event," said the commentator, as if he'd heard her question. "That's the head-butting contest— also known as the Battle of the Butts. . . ."

"We've got so little time!" squealed Gipsy. "What can we do?"

"Hang on," said Teggs grimly. He began to nose about the raptors' security room. "I'll bet it's round here somewhere. . . . Aha!" he cried, shoving his head into a cupboard. "Just what we need!"

"What have you found?" Gipsy asked breathlessly. "A way to defuse the bombs?"

"Nope—moss! It was part of the ransom, remember?" asked

Teggs. He pulled a massive green mouthful out of the cupboard. "I always think better on a full stomach." With that, he scoffed down the lot and let out an enormous, satisfied belch. "Now come on, Gipsy. No more dawdling—we've got a planet to save!"

Back on the *Sauropod*, high above the planet, Arx and Iggy were watching the countdown to the games on the scanner screen. Graceful pterodactyls soared through the air above the stadium with cameras in their long jaws. They were beaming all the action live to a hundred worlds through-out the dinosaur empire.

"Look," said Iggy, "Hank and Crank are first up to compete!"

"And here are two true head-butting heroes," said the commentator, *"two plucky stegoceras with the hardest heads of any herbivore around . . . Hank and Crank!"*

The stadium, crammed with thousands of excited dinosaurs, shuddered with a giant roar of approval. Even the dimorphodon flight crew on the *Sauropod* stopped work for a while, watching attentively from perches all about the flight deck.

One pterodactyl zoomed in to show Hank and Crank circling each other on all fours, heads lowered . . .

"Not long to go now, folks," came the commentator's voice. *"When the stadium clock strikes three times, the contest will begin. And I think we're in for some really explosive action today!"*

Teggs and Gipsy raced for the royal paddock. They knew they had to warn the kings and queens and cancel the contest.

They hurried down a long escalator lined with regal red carpet. Breathless, they approached the diamond-studded doors that led to the royal paddock.

Suddenly five stubby-headed carnotaurus stewards appeared from nowhere, blocking the way. The stewards' tiny eyes glinted beneath the short pointed horns on their eyelids.

"Can we help you?" asked one coldly.

"Even better," said another, "can we *eat* you?"

Teggs ignored him. "We need to get into the royal paddock," he panted.

"Oh, yeah?" The first carnotaurus wrinkled his nostrils. "You don't look like royalty to me."

"We have special passes," said Teggs. "Gipsy?"

The color drained from Gipsy's crest as she searched for them. "I've lost them!"

The stewards laughed, their tiny little forearms waggling with mirth. "You must think we hatched yesterday!" they cried.

Teggs glared at them and turned back to Gipsy. "You must have dropped them in the raptor enclosure. You know, when you sat on that security guard . . ."

He trailed off. The stewards narrowed their eyes still further.

"What were a couple of royal herbivores doing inside a raptor enclosure?" asked the first, leaning forward suspiciously. "Perhaps *you've* got something to do with the raptors not showing up at the games."

Teggs groaned in despair. "We don't have time for this!"

Outside, the pterodactyls were still zooming through the air with their TV cameras. The commentator's voice echoed from the stadium: "*The tension mounts! In just a few moments*

82

the great clock will chime . . . and Hank and Crank
will get butting!"

"*Please!*" cried Gipsy. "We have to get out
there and stop them!"

"Don't think so," snarled the second steward. "First you have to get out of *here*."

The five powerful predators advanced menacingly toward Teggs and Gipsy, drool
dripping from their jaws. . . .

Chapter Ten

DROPPING IN

"Sorry, guys," said Teggs as he lashed out at the nearest steward with his tail. "But I think you'll thank me later!" The carnotaurus was sent flying, and the other stewards leaped back in surprise. "Quick, Gipsy!" he yelled. "Inside!"

Together they burst into

the royal paddock. Close behind them came
the five stewards. Dinosaur kings and queens
gasped and shrieked as Teggs and Gipsy
pushed past them. They spilled drinks,
crushed crowns, and sent golden chairs scattering.

"Stop the contest!" Teggs yelled, dodging
the snapping jaws of the nearest carnotaurus.
"I'm a space captain!"

"Look!" Gipsy cried.

She was staring in horror at an enormous
video screen.

The pterodactyls had zoomed in on the great clock. It was edging ever closer toward three. They had only seconds to stop Hank and Crank from making the biggest bang in dinosaur history!

Suddenly Teggs had a brilliant idea.

"The ptero-dactyls, Gipsy!" he shouted, almost tramp-ling several queens as he dodged another steward. "The ones with the TV cameras! Maybe they can lift us out into the stadium!"

"It's worth a try, sir!" Gipsy nimbly hopped onto the back of a startled diplodocus. She whistled and clicked urgently at the flying reptiles high above them—just like she bossed about the dimorphodon on the *Sauropod*'s flight deck.

Teggs backed away from the angry carnotaurus stewards who had finally fenced him in. They advanced, closer and closer, jaws snapping, little hands twitching. . . .

Suddenly a dozen pterodactyls dived out of the sky. They dropped the TV cameras on the stewards' heads, and sent them sprawling.

Teggs grinned at Gipsy. "I'm glad you speak fluent pterosaur!"

"I told them what I'd do to them if they didn't help!" Gipsy winked. "I'm just glad they believed me!"

Gipsy clicked and whistled some more. A moment later Teggs felt the armored plates that ran down his back being gripped and lifted by twenty-four claws and twelve jaws.

The great clock chimed once. The sound was almost drowned out by the roar of the crowd.

"Quick!" yelled Teggs. Then his stumpy legs were kicking the air as he was lifted up, up into the sky.

The clock chimed twice.

Teggs gulped as he looked down. Gipsy was just a distant speck far below, but he thought he could hear her calling out, wishing him luck.

"Good work, guys," he called to his flapping friends. He just hoped they spoke his language. "Now, see those orange nutters with the hard heads? Take me there!"

The clock chimed for the third and final time.

"Hurry!" Teggs bellowed.

As the crowd clapped and cheered, Hank and Crank ran out into the stadium.

"Here we go, folks!" the commentator cackled over the loudspeakers. *"These hardheaded herbivores are ready for a bone-jarring skull-joust. I'm sure it'll be one we'll never forget!"*

"Flap faster, fellas!" Teggs was almost directly above the athletes now. . . .

Hank and Crank lowered their deadly heads. They were ready to charge. . . .

"Right!" roared Teggs. "Put me down! Quick!"

To his horror the pterodactyls did *exactly* as he'd asked—and simply let go of him.

With a yell of surprise Teggs began to plummet from the sky like a miniature meteor.

Beneath him in the stadium the stegoceras began to charge forward.

"Stop!" Teggs cried desperately. "You mustn't hit your heads!"

Perhaps Hank and Crank couldn't hear him.

Perhaps they just weren't listening.

They ran on, faster and

faster, the gap between them closing, *closing*...

And then the skydiving Teggs finally hit the ground—right between Hank and Crank! He gasped as the air was bashed from his body.

The shocked crowd fell utterly silent.

Hank and Crank were running too fast to stop. They crashed into Teggs's belly, then bounced backward.

"Ooof!" grunted Teggs as he screwed his eyes tightly shut. He waited for the inevitable blast of the bombs.

But nothing happened.

As he gingerly opened his eyes again, Teggs saw a worried hadrosaur bounding over to join him.

"Captain!" Gipsy cried. "Are you all right?"

"This must be how the meteor felt when it hit Earth!" groaned Teggs weakly.

Gipsy hugged him. "I thought it was all over when Hank and Crank ran into you!"

"Must be that moss I scoffed before setting off," said Teggs. "Made my stomach extra springy and squashy—so the bombs didn't go off!"

As the coos and chatter of the startled crowd began again, Teggs heard two weak groans on either side of him.

"Hank!" he gasped. "Crank! Are you guys okay?"

"I never read anything about a flying stegosaurus in the rules," Hank muttered. "But it's a cool idea!"

"Yeah, awesome!" Crank agreed feebly. "But can someone please get this tail off my face?"

Teggs was about to oblige when a massive menacing shadow fell over the stadium. It was pointed and curved like an enormous claw, scratching out the sun.

The crowd fell silent.

And Teggs and Gipsy found themselves staring up at the sinister shape of a raptor death-ship.

Chapter Eleven

THE FINAL CHALLENGE

"This is General Loki," an angry voice announced, booming out of the enormous spaceship. "I am Commander of the Seven Fleets of Death, ruler of the meat mines of Raptos, eater of—Well, you get the idea. Anyway—I bring an urgent message for Captain Teggs."

"Uh-oh," Teggs muttered. Gipsy tried to help him rise, but his legs were too bruised from the fall. He lay there helplessly, as if crushed into the ground by the weight of the ship's shadow.

"You've spoiled our evil plans, Captain," said Loki tetchily. "You've saved this entire miserable planet from destruction."

A giant gasp went up from the crowd.

"Yes, I said *destruction*! If I had my way, you would all be space dust by now! But this pea-brained fool has spoiled all my plans—"

The crowd cheered and whooped.

"But you shall not enjoy your victory for long!" Loki added in his most sinister voice.

As the words echoed round the arena, a large cannon slid slowly out from underneath the raptor ship. It swivelled until it was aimed directly at Teggs. He and Gipsy could only stare up at it helplessly.

But then another shadow fell. And when Teggs saw what was casting it, he grinned in amazement.

"This is the DSS *Sauropod*," Arx's voice boomed out from the ship's speaker system. "Perhaps you didn't hear, General Loki? The raptors are a no-show at this year's games—so get lost!"

With that, a volley of laser fire tore loose from the *Sauropod*. As the red and white lightning burned and crackled around the raptor ship, the whole crowd heard General Loki's howl of rage.

With an earsplitting sonic boom, Loki's death-ship was sent spinning away from the stadium. Soon it had vanished from view behind one of the six scarlet suns glowing in the sky.

"We did it!" cried Gipsy, her crest flushing bright red. "We saved the planet!"

"Ladies and gentlemen," announced the bewildered commentator over the speakers, *"it seems we owe a good deal today to Captain Teggs—a truly amazing astrosaur—and the crew of his fine ship, the DSS* Sauropod!*"*

The crowd burst into thundering cheers and applause as the DSS *Sauropod* flew slowly and gracefully off into orbit. Gipsy clapped too. Moments later medics appeared. They swiftly tended to Teggs and the dazed athletes beside him.

As he was hefted away on a stretcher, Teggs smiled proudly up at the shrinking shape of his ship. He raised both his front legs in a dinosaur salute.

Some time later Captain Teggs was back in his control pit, feasting on some of the finest ferns he had ever tasted. His legs felt much stronger, but he thought it best to take things easy for a while.

Beside him Gipsy was busy reading aloud all the thank-you messages they'd received.

"There's one here from Hank and Crank," she said happily. "The doctors have put their heads back to normal. But apparently they're really disappointed."

"Why?" wondered Teggs. "Because they couldn't take part in the games?"

"No." She chuckled. "Because they were hoping that exploding heads could become part of the sport!" She checked her readout. "Hey, there's even a note from King Carnotaurus here. He says he's very sorry his stewards tried to eat you."

"No harm done," said Teggs briskly, turning to Arx. "Which I hope is more than can be said for General Loki?"

The triceratops smiled. "Iggy gave the lasers a power boost—enough to knock that raptor ship clear out of orbit! There's no telling where they'll end up!"

"Actually," said Iggy slyly, "there *is*." He gave Teggs a wicked grin. "I took a look with the long-range scanners, Captain. And guess what! Loki's ship will be forced to land for repairs somewhere around here." Iggy turned on the scanner with his stiff little tail, and soon Teggs was staring at the green disc of a very familiar planet.

"Planet Sixty!" he beamed. "Really?"

"Serves them right," laughed Arx. "I wonder if that group of *T. rex*es is still there."

Gipsy grinned. "They'll certainly keep Loki busy for a while!"

"And what about us?" asked Iggy. "I like to be kept busy too!"

"Take it easy while you can," came a booming voice. Everyone looked up to see a crusty old barosaurus on the scanner screen.

"Admiral Rosso!" gasped Gipsy.

"That's right!" he beamed. "I just wanted to congratulate you all on a job well done."

"Thank you, sir," said Teggs.

"Thank *you*." The admiral nodded. "You've come through your first mission with flying colors."

"And flying stegosaurs, too!" whispered Gipsy, nudging Teggs in the ribs.

"We couldn't have done it without the *Sauropod*, sir," Teggs told him, helping himself to an extra big mouthful of delicious ferns. "She's a fine ship."

"And she has a fine crew," said the admiral with a smile. "And you know what? I have a hunch that somewhere out there, a new adventure's waiting . . . just around the corner."

Admiral Rosso's face faded from the screen.

Now the scanner showed the view outside the ship: the endless sparkle and darkness of deep space. Teggs stared at it dreamily. He couldn't wait to explore it all.

"Well," he said, "I think we should get going."

Arx raised a bony eyebrow. "Where to, Captain?"

"You heard the admiral—just around the corner!" Teggs winked at him. "Don't you know it's rude to leave an adventure waiting?"

TALKING DINOSAUR!
How to say the dinosaur names in this book . . .

ANKYLOSAURUS—
an-KI-loh-SORE-us

BAROSAURUS—
bar-oh-SORE-us

BRACHIOSAURUS—
brak-ee-oh-SORE-us

CARNOTAURUS—
KAR-noh-TORE-us

DIMORPHODON—
die-MORF-oh-don

DIPLODOCUS—
dih-PLOH-de-kus

EDMONTOSAURUS—
ed-MON-toh-SORE-us

HADROSAUR—
HAD-roh-sore

IGUANODON—
ee-GWAH-noh-don

MAIASAURA—
MY-ah-SORE-ah

ORNITHOMIMOSAUR—
OR-ni-thoh-MEE-moh-sore

PTERODACTYL—
teh-roh-DACK-til

PTEROSAUR—
TEH-roh-sore

SALTASAURUS—

sal-ah-SORE-us

STEGOCERAS—

ste-GOS-er-as

STEGOSAURUS—

STEG-oh-SORE-us

TRICERATOPS—

trie-SER-rah-tops

TYRANNOSAURUS—

tie-RAN-oh-SORE-us

VELOCIRAPTOR—

veh-LAH-si-RAP-tor

READ THE FIRST CHAPTER HERE!

Chapter One

THE EDGE OF EGG-STINCTION!

In a very big hall full of very big dinosaurs, a very big announcement was about to be made. The Hall of Learning on the planet Odo

Minor had never been more packed. Doctors, professors, scientists, TV cameras—they were all squashed up together. The sound of excited dinosaur chatter filled the hall. What was the big news? What had the great Professor Sog discovered now?

Two people in the hall already knew. And one of them didn't seem to care very much.

"I don't see why we had to come all this way!" grumbled Captain Teggs Stegosaur. "I haven't been in a learning hall since I passed my astrosaur exams!"

"Be patient, Captain," his

companion, Gipsy, whis-
pered. "As soon as the
talk's over, our mis-
sion can begin!"

"About time too,"
Teggs declared. He
was a captain in the
Dinosaur Space Service,
and he lived for adventure.
With his brave crew of astrosaurs
he traveled through space in the DSS
Sauropod, the finest ship in the Jurassic
Quadrant.

Gipsy, a stripy hadrosaug, was his communications officer. She and Teggs had come here
to escort Professor Sog back to the *Sauropod*—
along with some very special guests. . . .

She knew her crewmates would be busy up
in orbit. Arx Orano, Teggs's brainy triceratops
first officer, would be checking over the
Sauropod's systems. And Iggy Tooth, the tough

iguanodon engineer, would be stoking the ship's mighty engines.

Their latest voyage into outer space would be their longest yet.

"At last," cheered Teggs, making Gipsy jump. "Here comes Professor Sog now!"

Sog was a small twittery old creature who belonged to a species called compsognathus. The audience hooted and stamped their feet politely as the funny little figure walked onto the stage. He stopped beside a mysterious lumpy bundle hidden beneath a black blanket.

A great hush fell over the hall. The dinosaurs waited breathlessly for the professor's words.

Sog struggled to put on a small pair of spectacles. He had trouble reaching his head since his arms were so short. But finally he managed it, and he peered round at the curious crowd.

"Welcome, my friends," he cried. "You are about to hear of a most exciting discovery!"

A bright light started glowing above his head. Seconds later a hologram of a large long-necked dinosaur appeared. It looked a bit like a stegosaurus but with a longer neck and tail, and no spiky plates running down its back.

"This is a plateosaurus," said Sog. "Sweet, peaceful—and almost totally extinct."

"Extinct?" asked a puzzled journalist in the crowd.

Sog nodded sadly. "Their species has almost completely died out."

"Dined out?" asked Teggs, perking up. He was famous for his large appetite—some said it was the largest in the whole Dinosaur Space Service. "Dined out where? Can we come too?"

"Not dined out, *died* out!" groaned Gipsy.

Professor Sog continued his talk. "As you all know, we dinosaurs left Earth long ago. We escaped in spaceships before the meteor struck, never to return. In those days there were many plateosaurus. Nowadays there are hardly any left."

"Why?" someone called.

"Homesickness," said Sog simply. "At first they settled on a fine planet called Platus. But they didn't like it as much as Earth, so they tried to return." He shook his head sadly. "Their space fleet flew into a cosmic storm. Many of their ships were destroyed. The few survivors limped back to Platus . . . to find that *T. rex*es had taken over."

The audience murmured their disapproval.

"I remember reading about that," whispered Teggs. "The *T. rex*es wouldn't budge. There was a big battle."

Gipsy nodded sadly. "And the plateosaurus lost."

"Other vegetarian races came to their aid," the professor went on. "As you know, they joined together and formed the Dinosaur Space Service, to protect all plant-eaters. In the end they kicked the *T. rexes* off Platus. But the little planet had been almost ruined by war."

The hologram switched off above Sog's head. "The plateosaurus species never recovered from the tragedy. Today only a tiny handful survive." He shuffled closer to the black bundle beside him. "But now I bring new hope!"

He clamped his jaws down on the blanket and whipped it away. Beneath it was a pile of nine large white eggs. The audience burst out in gasps and hoots. Flying reptiles flapped nearer with their TV cameras to get a closer look. "Plateosaurus eggs!" cried the little professor. "Discovered in a wrecked space-ship far out in the Jurassic Quadrant. That ship was a victim of the cosmic storm. It has drifted through space for thousands of years. But the eggs survived—frozen completely!"

The great hall filled with excited mutterings.

Professor Sog held up his feeble arms for quiet. "As you know, when it comes to hatching, I am something of an expert. . . ."

"*Eggs*-pert, more like!" Teggs chuckled.

"I was asked to study these old, old eggs," said Sog proudly. "And now that the eggs have thawed out, I believe they will soon hatch! The plateosaurus race *will* live on!"

The audience cheered and stamped their feet so hard that the floor shook.

"That's where we come in!" cried Teggs, rising to his feet. He flexed his long, bony tail, and knocked two elderly triceratops off their stools. "Oops!"

Sog frowned at the commotion. "Is that Captain Teggs?"

"Speaking!" he called cheerily, as Gipsy helped up the doddery dinosaurs. "Hello, everyone. It's my mission to take the professor, the eggs, and two plateosaurus guardians to a far-off world called Platus Two. A place where their race can make a fresh start!"

Ka-Boom!

Suddenly the enormous wooden doors at the front of the hall were kicked open. The great hall rang with gasps of shock from the startled crowd.

"Is that a fact?"

Teggs narrowed his eyes. In the doorway

stood a dozen small, ugly creatures. Their small turtlelike heads bobbed about on scrawny necks.

One of the creatures darted toward the stage. "A fresh start for these lovely little hatchlings?" he sneered. He shoved Professor Sog aside. "I don't think so! Not now the oviraptors are here!"

"Oviraptors?" Teggs frowned.

"Uh-oh!" Gipsy turned to Teggs in alarm. "They're nest-raiders! Egg-stealers!"

"We've got to stop them!" yelled Teggs. But he was blocked in on all sides by shocked old dinosaurs.

"I am Prince Goopo, and these are my royal brothers!" The oviraptor snatched up a plateosaurus egg and caressed it with his long, bony fingers. "Eggs are our favorite food, and eggs as rare as *these* will make a meal fit for a king—*and* his princes!" He threw back his head and laughed. "Forget your mission, Captain Teggs. The only place these eggs are going is *into our bellies*!"

Read the rest of

The

Hatching Horror

to find out if Teggs can save the eggs!

What would you do if you discovered your teacher was from another planet?

Read all of Bruce Coville's bestselling series!

TOM SWIFT™
young inventor

He's smart, impossibly cool under pressure, and has more gadgets than he has time for—meet Tom Swift, Young Inventor!

From the creators of Nancy Drew and the Hardy Boys comes a series that's chock-full of adventure, high-tech gadgets, and even higher stakes. Look for a new Tom Swift adventure three times a year!

#1 INTO THE ABYSS
By Victor Appleton

#2 THE ROBOT OLYMPICS
By Victor Appleton

#3 THE SPACE HOTEL
By Victor Appleton

Meet Zack:

He's a genuine intergalactic space hero who fell out of the back of his own spaceship!

Join him and Omega Chimp on the silliest, zaniest, wackiest adventures this side of the Milky Way!

And coming soon:

The Adventures of Commander Zack Proton and the Warlords of Nibblecheese